Water of Life

Also by Kathy L. Brown

The Resurrectionist: A Novella (Sean Joye Investigations Series, Book One)

Water of Life

Kathy L. Brown

Otter Springs Publishing
St. Louis

ISBN 978-1-7330895-0-0

Otter Springs Publishing
St. Louis

To Dan, my first and biggest fan.

Acknowledgements

Thanks to my sensitivity reader, Laura Ritz of Writing with Eloquence (www.WritingWithEloquence.com), the Word Sisters, the Corner Coffeehouse Group, Patrick Brown, and Dan Brown.

I sat in the Judge's old Tin Lizzie and watched Callow Creek rise. Sure I'd had better days now, but at least I was out of the cold rain.

Brown waters, up two feet since I'd crossed this same bridge at dawn, pounded the Shawneeville Bridge trestles. As the car idled on the deserted mud lane, I pictured streams all over Southern Illinois breaking their banks in the November downpour and devouring every road back to St. Louis. I also pictured His Honor chewing me out over the late moonshine delivery.

My friend, the bootlegger Caleb Callow, hadn't shown up at the feedstore where we'd planned to meet. A bit concerned, I was heading to the backup rendezvous, an abandoned shack with a meat-roasting pit Caleb called a "bar-b-que."

I blew on my numb fingers and tried to recall any landmark that might help me find the right road. The country lanes all looked alike. No familiar businesses or distinctive brick walls, let alone street name placards, to help the poor traveler along. Just trees. Fences. Cows, but they moved around quite a bit, actually. Not a trustworthy landmark.

"Wouldn't I be obliged for a bit of a sign as to which pig path is the turnoff?" I don't know whether I spoke to God or Saint Anthony. Most likely, the empty landscape. As best I could tell from my life to that point, God couldn't spare me the time of day. Saint Anthony? Well, he's a busy man.

As I eased the Model T toward the bridge, Caleb's lady friend, Maebelle, scrambled up the rocky creekbank to the left and ran in front of the car. Mud spattered her and the windscreen as I slammed the brake pedal.

"Stop! Stop the car." Maebelle pounded on the hood. "Sean, help us." She fumbled with the door latch and scrambled into the passenger side. "Help Caleb." As always, her voice was rough and strained, as if it hurt her to speak.

I'm not even sure Maebelle is actually her name; it didn't seem to fit her, somehow. But Caleb called her that, and she answered. Sometimes. With sleek black hair, sharp cheekbones, and a soft, red-brown complexion, she was beautiful, despite, or maybe because of, the fact she dressed like she'd robbed a clothesline. Today was no exception. She swam in a thin calico frock several sizes too big, the skirt cinched up with some sort of table linen. Against the rain, she wore a man's flannel shirt and galoshes.

Maebelle's scent of damp earth on a hot summer's day filled the cramped compartment and my frozen head as well. The car, the rain, the cold—my sense of myself—everything fell away as she smiled at me.

But losing track of who and where you are, pleasant as it might be in the moment, ain't wise. A faerie woman named Éire, back in the Irish Free State, had glamoured me once, and it felt much like spending time with Maebelle. Americans think faeries ain't real. Or else that they're tiny, harmless creatures, just the subject of amusing fables from the old country: That's all shite. They're real, alright.

With Maebelle so near, I tottered on the brink again, until the car rolled forward. Startled, I mashed the brake. "Jesus Mary and Joseph, woman. Wouldn't you be giving me a minute to park the car?"

Everything was always a crisis with Maebelle. Well, a crisis or a bit of craic—a lark. Often both at the same time. I nosed the car over to the side of the road and set the parking brake. The interruption gave me a chance to steel myself to her charms.

"Slow yourself down now. Revenuers got Caleb?" That would explain his absence and had been my chief worry.

She shook her head. Then nodded. Then shrugged.

"Could you be a bit more specific, then?"

She tilted her head and smiled.

The car didn't feel cold at all anymore. I reminded myself that Caleb and her were in love. Whatever I felt for either of them wasn't half so fine. "Tell me what scared you."

Her face clouded. "Gunshot."

"Who was shot? Where?"

"In cabin. Loud voices." She choked out the words. "He felt danger. I could hear it."

"You're not hurt, are you?" My eyes slid over the baggy dress, the neckline revealing more than a flash of her breasts. She didn't look hurt. "Caleb was shot?"

Maebelle shrugged. "Maybe. And he was so angry."

She'd climbed in my car ten minutes ago, and I still didn't know anything for sure except that Caleb had a problem involving gunplay. "Did you see what happened?"

She started to turn away but changed her mind and slapped me. My face was so frozen the sting felt good.

I grabbed her wrist. "I'm dense. I know. Talk to me."

"I was outside. I heard voices from the cabin."

"How many different voices?" The revenuers traveled in packs and tended to enlist the local sheriff, if they could find him. It could've been quite a crowd.

"Caleb was loud. Angry." Maebelle shrugged again. "Then one gunshot."

"And you didn't see who fired the gun?" My money was on Caleb. The man shot with sniper-trained accuracy and no hesitation. But this tale didn't add up. For one thing, I couldn't imagine how revenuers had sneaked up on him. Unless Maebelle wasn't outside at all, and she'd distracted him. On purpose.

Maebelle was watching the windscreen wipers as they squeaked back and forth. Would she betray Caleb to accomplish her own ends? She didn't have her own ends, as far as I could tell.

"You weren't ever in the cabin?"

She shook her head. "No. Not see. Caleb made—his sound—" Her words petered away into a throaty gibberish.

"OK. He knew he was in danger. Makes sense, since next thing you heard was a gunshot. Can you show me the place?"

She nodded and before I knew it, she'd pulled me down the muddy bank and into the woods. We followed Callow Creek upstream toward its source at Otter Springs. The rain slowed to a mist, tap-tapping on the oak leaves high overhead.

"And where would we be going, then?" I said.

Maebelle ignored my question and ran ahead, up the deer trail.

I stopped. I had to know a bit more, before I followed her any further.

Eventually she noticed and hurried back to tug on my sleeve.

I caught her hand and made her look me in the eyes. "Could you have tipped them off? Not on purpose, but mistakes happen."

She chewed her lower lip for a moment and then opened her mouth to speak.

"I can hear y'all out there," an old woman shouted at us from atop the ridge.

At the voice, Maebelle froze, eyes wide. Then she turned and fled without a word.

"Damn." Too late for stealth. I was well aware of the noise I'd made as I tripped and stumbled along the frozen flint path.

A cabin perched on the crest of the ridge, but I didn't even know if it was where Maebelle had been headed. I'd assumed the arrest, if that was what happened, was at Caleb's own place, a shack for shelter and supplies near his still. I'd never been there, but he'd mentioned it.

"Maebelle," I called after her, "is this the cabin?" She didn't reappear or answer. The more I thought about it, the more I suspected we'd arrived at Caleb's old family homestead where his granny now lived alone. He'd pointed it out once. Of course, I'd been quite turned around at the time.

A shell click-clacked into a shotgun's chamber. I knew that sound well enough and dove for cover behind a pile of lichen-covered boulders. My panted breath hung in the November air. And ain't that what comes from soft living? Riding around in automobiles all day took a man's strength as sure as sitting in prison for six months.

"Git on outta here." The old woman's voice was coarse. "It's mine now."

Although I could hear her, I could hardly see her through the dense wooded hillside above me. What I did see, most particularly and quite well, was the shotgun hefted to her shoulder and pointed square at the rocky outcrop that shielded me. For the moment.

It stood to reason she couldn't actually hit me. Caleb had described his grandmother as at least eighty, and I was a good fifty yards away. Nevertheless, I felt her bead right on me and that she had no qualms about dropping me where I cowered. Just another missing city slicker.

Maebelle had reported a gunshot, and here was granny ready to shoot me. But everyone in these hills seemed to carry a weapon around all the time. The old woman was likely to be afraid of whoever had arrested Caleb. Or she greeted all visitors with death threats.

"Sorry," I shouted. "But ain't it important now? I'm—" I wasn't quite sure what to say. Caleb actually knew my name, but the few other folks I'd met in this little town did not. They thought I was some Welshman named Jones from Chicago. Just a precaution in my line of work. But Caleb might have mentioned me to her. "Sean Joye. A friend of your grandson." I stuck my hands in the air and stood up.

"Hold it right there."

The clouds parted for a moment, and a ray of sunlight glinted off the barrel. Through the trees, I saw her limp across the clearing in front of the cabin.

"Which grandson?"

I was worried about Caleb, impatient to get back to the city with my cargo, and tired from the climb. But demands for information from her seemed the wrong play.

"Caleb Callow, ma'am," I said, in my best tea-with-gran tone. "He was to deliver some goods to Holmes's feedstore this morning. Items for a St. Louis customer." That customer being the Judge.

Last spring, in America but a few weeks, I'd been nicked doing something stupid. Judge Dolan— "the Judge" to the entire city— had dismissed the charges, lent me a quarter for a haircut, and pressed this errand-runner job upon me.

When I'd inquired about Caleb at the feedstore, Holmes had hazarded a guess that he might be out with Maebelle. I allowed that was possible. But, no matter his devotion to her, business was business, and Caleb was a man of business.

"What, he weren't there?" said the old woman.

"Ma'am, I'm lowering my arms, 'cause they hurt, and I'm coming on ahead, 'cause I'm cold—"

A spray of buckshot spattered the oak leaves overhead. A squirrel dropped at my feet. I drew a breath, and my heart began to beat again. "Nobody in town's seen him all day."

"Come on then. Bring the critter."

"Yes, ma'am." I picked up the animal, warm and plump with fat stored for winter, and trotted up the path toward the cabin.

The creek ran down the hill and blocked my way. Its pebbles shone like ladies' jewelry in a shop case, and mossy stepping stones spanned the flow. A pretty place, even on such a cold, gray day. An oak, tall and wide, grew out of the opposite bank. I'm Belfast city born and bred, but even I recognized its age. It must have been an old tree a hundred years ago, when America was young.

A family of river otters yelped at one another, swooped down the creekbank, and dove into the deep pool formed in the oak's root basin. Startled by the splashes, I almost fell into the water as I picked my way across the rocks. Their diving-tag game was funny at first, but its goal seemed to be to break the surface as near me as possible and fling water on my coat. I scrambled up the creekbank and onto the path to the old lady's log cabin.

Pines winked at me in the afternoon light, and oak leaves chattered in a blast of cold out of the west. A shiver ran up my back. I felt as if the old woods itself had spotted me and didn't much like what it saw, but it was no time for fancy. Just colder weather coming on, that was all.

I guess the old woman saw me shiver. "Someone just walked over your grave, boy." From the small flat clearing in front of the cabin, she trailed my movement with the shotgun, quite accurately considering the fact she was gasping for air. She stood almost as tall as Caleb, which gave her a good six inches on me.

She didn't seem to feel the cold at all, although her voice was hoarse. "Hope you's right with the Lord."

I stopped and raised my arms again, still grasping the squirrel by the tail. "I don't mean to pry, ma'am, but could I fetch you a chair?"

"Don't you never mind. I expect I know when I need to rest."

I smiled, all cheerful and friendly, like I was held at gunpoint every day and didn't mind it a bit. Actually, I could well do without the experience ever again. Old lady or not, her shotgun appeared to be in good working order.

The cold rain resumed, and I wished I'd had a chance to button my overcoat before this standoff began. "Wouldn't you want to be putting away the gun and for us to talk indoors?"

Moist tendrils of white hair frizzed around her face. Mud spattered her brown calico dress's hem, and the cuffs were soiled. But the shotgun held my attention.

"My, but you's the runt of the litter. And barely outta short pants. I'd peg you for a coal miner, but for the slick gitup."

"Uh, thank you. I think." I'm actually five foot seven and a half and don't think I look particularly young for my age, but there you are. I'd certainly heard that before. Well, not the coal miner part. "I'm twenty-three and a veteran," I continued. I didn't see the need to tell her for what army. The Irish struggle for freedom was of little interest to Americans, so intent they were to forget the Great War.

"So, I need to know—" I began, then thought better of blurting out my questions. I knew little about Caleb's grandmother, except that she scared Maebelle. And Caleb, too, a little. "If I can get a hot cuppa tea? Ain't the rainy day turned brisk, now?"

The old lady seemed to waiver. Would the satisfaction of shooting me be worth the work of hiding my body? She pointed at the porch steps with the gun muzzle.

"Well, be in, be in."

I mounted the stairs, hands still high and squirrel at the ready. Foothold animal traps draped the rails on either side of the stairs. Pelts, many stretched and pinned over narrow boards, dried on the deep porch. Blood's coppery tang hung on the air.

She followed me into the cabin and put the gun in a rack by the door, then extended her hand. "I'm Lutra Callow."

I shook it. "Sean Joye, Miss Lutra. Pleased to meet you. I guess you was expecting someone else."

"I'll make some coffee. Ain't got no tea. And you'll eat dinner."

"I wouldn't want to be putting you out. And I really should be hunting up Caleb, if he's not here."

"Praise Jesus you care about my boy. But a man's gotta eat." She indicated a low table. "In my house, leave your weapons over there." The table was bare, but for a Bible, a lantern in front of the window, and a beautiful fur heaped on the end farthest from the door.

"What makes you think I've a weapon?"

Miss Lutra was sorting through a drawer of camphor-scented fancy work. "You ain't no total fool, I reckon."

"So, Caleb's not here?"

She pulled a crisp linen apron from the bottom of the pile, gave it a shake, and tied it around her waist. Embroidered daisies dotted the bib and hem. "Can't you help an old lady for a spell? We can talk about him presently."

"Of course." I hadn't much hoped she'd simply tell me the revenuers had arrested Caleb right there in the kitchen, or that she'd even give me directions to the still. These hillfolk survived by suspicion. They were smart that way. "I get you. Silence is golden."

From Cork to Derry City, town to countryside, informants were bigger threats to Irish independence than the British Army, the Black and Tans, and the B-Special Constables combined. Just two years ago, back in 1921, an informant killed my men in an ambush at Lappinduff Mountain, as sure as if she'd shot them herself. I was still half numb with the betrayal, though the traitor was dead, and the war done.

"Don't mumble, boy. Speak up."

"Sorry. What do you need me to do?"

"Gimme that there varmint and bring in some water and wood." I handed the animal over, and she slammed the still-twitching squirrel onto a wooden cutting board and produced a large knife and a couple of turnips.

And she was right about me not being a total fool. I *didn't* go into the backwoods unarmed. I removed my Webley from its shoulder holster and lay it on the table. She wouldn't consider the folding knife in my pocket a weapon, would she?

Throughout our conversation, I'd had more than a bit of trouble not staring at the pelt draped across the table. Now my fingers strayed to it. I felt compelled to stroke the dark, smooth fur. It was the most beautiful thing in the world at that moment.

"A nice fur, there," I said. "What kind is it?"

Miss Lutra tightened her grip on the knife before looking up. "Otter."

"Make you a fine—" How would an elderly mountain woman wear a fur piece? Not a stole, or a muff, surely? "Collar or—hat."

She made no effort to hide her disgust at my fashion ignorance, grabbed the fur, and stuffed it in a drawer.

With the pelt out of sight, my mind turned back to Caleb. I could at least check the property. "Beg pardon, ma'am. I'll see to that water and wood."

She nodded, and I went out into the barnyard behind the cabin.

I carried in two buckets of water from the creek, then addressed the woodpile. A long-handled spade leaned against it, but I'd need an ax to split kindling. Finding one was a good pretense for an outbuilding search.

I slipped inside the dry-rotted barn and inhaled the sweet decay of alfalfa as my eyes adjusted to the semidarkness. A donkey and a goat occupied the only animal stall and looked up from the manger before them.

"And ain't it a foul day, gents? Sorry. I mean, lady—" I tipped my hat to the donkey. "*And* gent. Mind if I look about a bit?"

The donkey swished her tail, and the goat resumed munching the hay.

"I'll take that as a welcome in." I commenced my search. The barn yielded a sooty kerosene lantern, a pair of overalls, and a cot with a bedroll, ripe with sweat, corn squeezings, and tobacco. Caleb had slept here, and recently.

As I pondered my friend, his smell, and his fate, light arced across the floor. Maebelle stood in the open doorway, shivering in the cold. She eyeballed the animals for a long moment and then clomped in her heavy galoshes across the dirt floor to me.

"Fur. She has skin—"

"They do a lot of trapping here. You must know that."

She stomped her foot. "My pelt. In the cabin."

"Yours? The fine one she has inside belongs to you?"

She nodded, then looked up at me, more serious than I'd ever seen her. "Get it for me? She must not have it." Her raw voice was almost a growl.

"Are you sure? How would she—" I looked Maebelle in the eyes, and she turned away.

She wasn't telling me plenty, but that's not the same as lying. "I'll try. But I'm a bit more concerned about finding your man right now. And how did granny—"

She'd been sniffing around among his things while I talked and now lay on his narrow cot with the blanket up against her face.

"OK. I'll try. But Miss Lutra won't just hand it over if I ask. Maybe I can slip it out to the porch while she's cooking dinner."

I couldn't tell if Maebelle heard me. She'd curled up in a ball with Caleb's bedding and appeared to be asleep.

I continued my search for any sign of Caleb shooting someone, getting shot himself, or being arrested. The toolshed held tools. The chicken coop held chickens. The outhouse was a two-seater.

The burn barrel smoked from a smoldering mound of pine cones and trash. I fished out the charred remains of coarse cloth with the tip of my folding knife. It was shaped something like an apron, I supposed.

With an ax from the toolshed I split kindling and restocked the box on the cabin's porch. Then I puttered about a bit drinking black coffee, as Miss Lutra rattled pots and pans. I found little evidence of Caleb or any sort of struggle in the cabin. Also, no crooked moonshine account ledgers, threatening messages from his bookie, or court summons.

I'd had a bad feeling about Caleb since I started the trek up the mountain and couldn't shake it. He could have been nicked. Very likely, given Maebelle's story. I glanced out the window and hoped he was somewhere safe, not sitting in the jailhouse at the county seat. Or worse.

"What do you think of Caleb's lady?"

With a whack of the knife, Miss Lutra beheaded the squirrel. "There ain't no lady."

So she didn't know Caleb was keeping company with Maebelle. Or maybe didn't want to know. Or the denial might be a cover for stealing the pelt. "Sorry. I must be thinking of someone else."

As Miss Lutra dismembered our dinner, I finished my search of the cabin, acutely aware of the otter pelt in the chest of drawers. Natural enough I told myself, since I studied on when and how to lift it. But truth be told, I wanted to touch it again.

"You do a lot of hunting and trapping, Miss Lutra?"

She looked over at the fancywork drawer, then glanced at me. "It's the menfolk's work. They like to use my big porch for dressing the pelts." Miss Lutra was up to her elbows in some sort of dough. "And don't be bothering me while I'm cooking."

"I was just wondering—"

"I'll visit with you over dinner. Find some way to make yourself useful. Or sit with the

Good Book for a spell." She turned her back to me and made a show of concentration over the dinner preparations.

"Yes, ma'am." Obedient ever, I examined photos, the fireplace, and the family Bible, all the while with one eye on her.

But the Good Book had no words of wisdom for me that day. I replaced it on the lace doily near the oil lamp and positioned myself near the chest of drawers. Miss Lutra was intent on her cooking. Now was as good a time as any to get Maebelle's pelt back to her.

As the old lady opened the stove door to shove in more wood, I opened the drawer where she'd put the fur. Smooth and sleek, it begged to be stroked. I fought hard against an impulse to keep it. Surely Maebelle owed me something, all the trouble she'd put me to.

But I left it out on the porch and chose a similar pelt off a drying board. I scooped up an armload of wood as well as the replacement pelt and brought them inside. The switch was smooth, and I hoped Miss Lutra wouldn't be able to tell the difference. I sure could, though.

* * *

Letting old ladies feed me hasn't failed me yet. The stew and bread smelled great. My stomach growled as I sat down at the oak-plank dining table, and I realized I hadn't eaten all day.

Miss Lutra invited me to say grace over our meal, but apparently found my "For these thy gifts make us truly thankful" a poor effort and jazzed up the prayer with a blessing on the squirrel, the forest, the other animals of the forest, the creek, the farmland, Caleb—"who is lost from us but will be delivered whole and sound, if not now, at the final trumpet," me, my people, her people, and herself. Although mostly focused on my rumbling stomach, at the final "amen" I remembered not to cross myself, the Church of Rome not so very popular in these parts.

Miss Lutra had filled out the scant meat from a single squirrel with potatoes and turnips, and the meal was quite tasty. Between mouthfuls of hot stew, only marred by the occasional buckshot pellet, I said, "I don't mean to be abrupt, ma'am, but was Caleb here today or not?"

The old lady cut off a hunk of hot bread with her enormous knife and wiped her bowl with it, sopping up the peppery gravy. "You ain't from around here, are you, Mr. Sean Joye? Sound like you could even be from over the waters."

"Do I now? Does that make a matter where Caleb went?" Through the tiny window, I could see dark clouds full of snow gathering low over the woods. The otters were quiet. I wondered if Maebelle was still in the barn or if she'd recovered her stolen property and moved on. "Or does it make a matter of what you'll tell me?"

Miss Lutra spread a bit of blackberry jam on her bread and ate it. "Old Enoch Callow came from over there, too. Scotch-Irish. He made his way to Kentucky and raised up a big family. His youngest boy, James William, he got him a good education back East, trained up to be a preacher. He settled in these hills."

Her face softened, and she actually smiled as she watched the fire dance. "He were a fine figure of a man. He'd a beard and hair the color of sugar maples, just at the hard frost. And tall. Goodness, the man would've had to stoop to stand in *this* cabin! Broad-shouldered—"

She seemed to have forgot I was there, for a moment, then noticed me and stopped her story short. "So they say."

"Why'd he come here?"

"James William needed elbow room. When he got this far, he found a girl to marry." She pushed back from the table and rose to limp into the kitchen.

"Must be a good story in that."

She came back to the table with a pie. "She weren't nothing special. Just a girl. Her Pa were the—well, white folks say, 'medicine man.' That ain't quite the right word."

"The healer?"

She shook her head. "More like the preacher. But not like a white-man preacher. Not like James William."

"A priest, then."

Miss Lutra scowled. "I guess. But not one of your Church of Rome idolaters."

I smiled. "I wonder what the priest thought about his girl joining the competition."

She shrugged and cut a slab of pie and put it in my stew bowl. "Don't matter. Those people is all gone now."

"What about—" I remembered not to talk about Maebelle. "Haven't I seen a few Shawnee folks around here?" Caleb, for instance, traced his family back to Tecumseh himself.

"Well, there's them, like us Callows, what had an ancestor from one of the clans way back up the family tree. You can see it on their faces, sometimes. But those Shawnee people and the Osage. The Illini. All them had to go away, reservations in Kansas and Oklahoma or some such place. Long time ago."

"Caleb was proud of his line to Tecumseh." We'd spent a long, cold night together in September, holed up in a cave: Swapping stories, drinking too much, and waiting out revenuers who blocked the road back to town. To hear him talk, Caleb's ancestor had nearly halted America's westward march single-handed, until the Battle of Tippecanoe destroyed Tecumseh's capital city.

Miss Lutra snorted. "Don't know where he got that idea. Our folks mighta *known* Tecumseh, to speak to in passing, but we sure weren't no kin."

Poteen could've lubricated my friend's story a bit and maybe spiced up my recollection of the tale. People say and do things under the influence they normally wouldn't even consider. "Caleb said the first people are still here, if you knew where to look."

She snorted. "He didn't know much. They ain't here no more."

I finished the apple pie in silence, reliving my most recent brush with death and sin. Hiding in the cave was a fine plan, until someone tipped the agents as to where we were. How we'd survived that firefight, I still didn't understand.

I carried my bowl and the cast-iron stewpot on the stove over to the wash basin. "I guess you Callows are what's left of your Shawnee clan, in these parts, anyway, because of your ancestor." I rubbed the lye soap bar on a rag and wiped out the stew bowl, then dipped it in the water. "And that was good stew. And the best pie I ever ate. Thank you, ma'am."

"Leave that pot be. You'll ruin it. I'll wipe it out later." With a sigh, Miss Lutra moved over to the hearth and lowered her weight into a rocker.

"Sure ain't I had the washing up for my gran since I could stand on a stool at the sink?" Careful of the long-seasoned cast iron, I cleared the last bits of gravy from the pot with the rag. "She made a fine lamb stew in a pot like this, every Sunday." I poured in a bit of water and set the pot on the hot stove to loosen a few cooked-on remnants.

Miss Lutra watched me and then nodded her head, as if she'd come to some decision.

Now she's going to tell me something helpful I thought, leaving the stewpot to stand behind her chair.

"I want you to have it," she said, motioning to the pot on the stove. "It has a lid around here, somewheres. I'll find it."

"Thank you, Miss Lutra. You don't have to do that." I rested my hand on her shoulder. She didn't pull away. "Now, about Caleb. He's contracted to provide a dozen jugs of whiskey every couple of months to a certain person in St. Louis. Poteen or not, his whiskey is the best. Better than legit brands like Canadian Club, even."

She didn't answer.

The room grew darker, gloaming time near. I pulled up a footstool and sat in front of her.

Miss Lutra's face was a smooth mask, eyes staring at the fire. She rocked back and forth real slow.

"At home," I said, "we call it uisce beatha. The 'water of life.' And maybe it *is* the water here, or something, that makes it so good. But Caleb just didn't show up this morning. I'm worried. Somebody thought they heard him arguing—"

"Who? Where?"

"Don't matter. And I don't exactly know. I assumed at the still."

While I spoke, Miss Lutra took a tin from the mantle with shaking hands and cut off a small tobacco plug. She sat again and commenced to chew. She offered the tobacco to me.

I shook my head as I showed her I had a pipe.

"My grandson, he said you's a papist."

Ah, I thought. Caleb *had* mentioned me.

She worked the chaw. "But good in a fight. He seemed to think a lot of you."

I tamped my tobacco in the pipe and lit it. "We've had a scrap or two, me and Caleb."

"I'd love to see you open your heart to Jesus as your personal savior."

"If I did, would you tell me where Caleb is?"

"The two ain't got nothing to do with each other." Miss Lutra leaned forward to spit in the fire. "He's been distracted, roaming the woods. Talking about haints and the like. Maybe the 'shine's addled his brain. But he ain't been here in days." Her tough face broke, and she looked every one of her years. "Something got to him. There's powers in the woods. Dangerous powers. I don't know what to do, except sit here and pray."

The only dangerous powers I knew of that loitered about in the woods were faeries and fae creatures of their ilk. Best to call them the "Good People," if talk about them you must: They take offense all too easily.

Although spiriting a good-looking young fella away is just the sort of thing they'd do, it didn't make any sense. As best I knew, I'd left the Good People behind in Ireland. And Maebelle had heard a real argument. And a real gunshot. But I played along with Miss Lutra's story for the moment. "The other side of the Veil is dangerous, to be sure."

She stopped rocking her chair and looked away. Maybe she'd glimpsed the other side, too, sometime in her long life.

"But the Good People ain't skulking in your woods. They can't cross the ocean." That's what I liked to tell myself, anyway. I switched to a more direct tactic. "Have any of your people gone up to his still? Could he be there?"

"They're scared of haints and such." Miss Lutra resumed rocking and chawing.

"What about checking at the jail?"

"Ah, they'd all be afraid of a run-in with the law."

I didn't understand her casual attitude. "His whereabouts matter more to me than his kin?"

Miss Lutra spat into the fire again. "I'd say what matters to y'all is his whiskey."

That hurt, a little bit. "Why don't we say Caleb matters to me, and his whiskey matters to my boss. He didn't say nothing about going away? Or plans for today?"

"Well, not to me." She shot up out of the rocker and grabbed the poker. She attacked the fire, then said over her shoulder, "You got a wife, Mr. Joye? Young 'uns at home, back in the city? Or over the water?"

Maybe she smelled that weakness on me. I watched the flames vaporize the pine resin oozing from the logs. "My wife, Norah, died. Her and the child with her." Not telling everything ain't the same as lying.

I felt a bony hand grasp my arm. "Take it to the Lord in prayer."

"I've said everything I've got to say to Him about it." I looked up. Miss Lutra actually smile at me. She was laughing, almost.

"Now 'tis time to listen."

In a sudden need to justify myself, I dug the hole deeper. "My dear bride was a selfish, lying, traitorous bitch. If I hadn't been in jail at the time—" I'd acquired a bit of fancywork off a table and was twisting it within an inch of its life.

Miss Lutra held my gaze steady. "What a crock," she snorted. "Everyone wants to kill what they love, in some way, some time. We's all sinners, but for the grace of God."

I suppose that's true. I smoothed out her doily as best I could and put it back. Rain tapped on the window. Gesturing at the row of mantel photos, I said, "Your family, there?"

"Grandchildren, mostly." Her face clouded. "My man died long ago, before all these here snappy shots and the like." She leaned back in the rocker. The late afternoon had sneaked in on us, and the room was dark, except for the fire and the shadows it threw, slapping and playing across the hearth.

"I were a widow woman a long time. Then I fell in powerful love again, like a silly young thing, with a man passing through these hills. He done up and left me." She gave me a reproachful look. "City sharpie."

"Tisk, tisk." I was all sympathy and regret, on behalf of city sharpies everywhere. "Did you never remarry?"

"It ain't good to be alone. I married with old Noble Callow. A good man, and his wife had just died and left him with a houseful of young 'uns." She ran her bent fingers though her hair, lost in thought. "The Lord should take me. Maybe now."

I was still caught in the recollection of things best left alone. Norah's image pressed through the cracks in my attention.

The fire ejected a spray of sparks, and a log rolled off the andiron. Miss Lutra repositioned it with the tongs. "And Jesus sent you to find my grandson. I don't know what to make of that."

"Let's be finding him, then. Go up to the still." But I needed her help. The location was a guarded family secret, and I had no idea how to find it.

Her eyes narrowed. "He ain't done told you where the still is, did he?"

"No, ma'am. But aren't you going to tell me now, as I'm the only one you got to hunt down Caleb?"

"Well, it's nigh unto dark, too dark for you to find the still."

A sharp noise intruded from the porch. Miss Lutra went to the window and looked out. "Where's my pelt?" She upended the dresser drawer, dumping the animal skin I'd switched with the fine pelt to the floor, not fooled for a moment.

She glared at me. "Where's my skin?" I expected her to tear my head off any second.

"Right there on the floor, ma'am." I inched toward the door.

Miss Lutra snatched my Webley off the table and launched herself out the front door and onto the porch. She leaned over the rail, staring hard into the woods. A fine freezing mist filled the air. Then she turned, the gun leveled at my chest. "You're gonna git it from her. Now."

"Don't you think we should be more concerned about finding Caleb?"

"He's beyond worldly cares, mister. Safe with his Heavenly Father. But I—I need my pelt. Now git. I'm sure she run off with it to the creek."

"Beyond worldly cares" sounded like Caleb was dead, and "she run off" sounded like Miss Lutra knew about Maebelle all along. I didn't like my mind leaping in that direction. Not at all. And why was she more concerned with a disputed fur piece than Caleb's fate and whereabouts?

"OK." I tried to keep my suspicions out of my voice. "I'll get it back." The steps were already glazed. "You stay here. Don't try to walk on the ice."

"You'd like that, wouldn't you? I was running on sheet ice before you was born. Git going."

She at least allowed me to put on my coat and hat before shoving me out into the sleet. I clung to the wooden handrail and took the steps one at a time. "Couldn't you just put away the gun, Miss Lutra? Before someone gets hurt?"

She chuckled. I supposed she'd been marching people across sheet ice at gunpoint before I was born as well.

I slid across the clearing and skidded down the path to the creek as quickly as I could. I hoped to outdistance her, but she kept up fine. As I crossed the creek's stepping stones, I heard a commotion of grunts and yelps from upstream.

Something of interest to the otters floated in the water. Despite the gloom and sleet, I could see it was a man's body. It drifted toward the pool where the otters had sported a few hours before. Although the man was caked in mud, a yellow kerchief was visible around his neck. I'd seen that rag before. Tied to a particular door handle, it was a signal that the goods were ready for pickup.

Caleb. I looked back at Miss Lutra. Her mouth hung open in surprise. For a moment, I was heartened.

"How'd he end up in the creek?" she said. She motioned me toward the body with my gun. "Best pull him out."

I scrambled down the creekbank to retrieve Caleb. As much as I wished revenuers had done this, I knew his granny was somehow responsible. My soul hurt for the weight Miss Lutra carried. I know killing's weight.

I struggled to get a firm grasp on Caleb, finally pulling the body up the otters' slide by the bib of his overalls. I lay him on a pile of leaves. It was safe to assume the shotgun blast that took off most of his face was the cause of death. The stiffness hadn't passed yet. He'd been killed within the day, most likely.

I looked up at the woman trembling over me with my own revolver. "Let's get in where it's warm and talk about this—accident. You must be a bit shook."

"We came out here to git my pelt back, and that's what you's gonna do." She waved the gun, motioning me to stand. "My boy there's in a better place, and I'll be joining him soon."

An otter poked its head through the thin ice around the tree roots and climbed out of the water. Miss Lutra drew in a sharp breath. The otter shook the water from its pelt and regarded the body, then me, with solemn brown eyes. It looked up at the old woman.

"I'm sorry," Miss Lutra said to the animal. "I didn't mean to kill him. But I had to have it."

The forest stilled. The wind, rain, and sleet stopped. Snowflakes twinkled and winked like sparks in the gray-green of dusk. But just for the moment. A second later we were all three pelted with ice again.

Taking advantage of Miss Lutra's crazy spell, I made a play to get my gun. But at my first movement, she pressed the revolver against my forehead and continued to talk to the otter. "It's the only way out for me, don't you see? I can't die in this form, can't cross the Jordan. Gimme it, if you care about this one at all."

The animal seemed to consider Miss Lutra's words, then nuzzled about my ankles like a cat. I was puzzled as hell. The old woman's face looked like Christmas morning. I didn't know what she was so happy about, but I saw another chance to grab my gun.

Just then the otter wobbled up on its hind legs. It shrugged its left shoulder, and its pelt seemed to loosen. With a twist of the right shoulder, the fur came right off, like a lady wiggling out of a cardigan. Wind blew sleet in my eyes, and I blinked at just the wrong second, I guess. When I could see again, the fur was pooled around her ankles. The otter was Maebelle, naked and shivering. She gathered the pelt and handed it to Miss Lutra. "Mine. My skin. Mine." She watched the pelt in Miss Lutra's hand as if the old woman held her soul.

At home, we call them selkies: The sealfolk. Oh, they're Good People, too, the fae that live along the coastline, shedding their sealskins to sport on the beach as fine women. A human may take one as his bride, hold her skin as dowry, but she will always and forever long for the sea. Such a romance generally ends in tears.

Miss Lutra rubbed the pelt against her face as the sleet changed over to thick, wet snowflakes.

"Let me give her my coat, Miss Lutra." Faerie or not, Maebelle was turning blue from the cold.

The old woman nodded.

I eased out of my coat and held it open for Maebelle to come to me.

"She's caught you, too, Mr. Joye. Just like she did Caleb."

I'd leaped to a few conclusions and tried one out on her. "Like that clan priest's daughter caught your ancestor, James William?"

Shame and rage chased one another across Miss Lutra's face. "You trying to git yourself killed?" But my heavy gun shook in her hand. "It weren't like that all."

"How was it? If anything like Caleb and Maebelle, a curious glance turned to a passing fancy, and that fancy somehow grew into love." In for a penny, in for pound, I yammered on. "James William's bride was a faerie woman, with a shifting nature, I bet. The selkie-otters here and you Callows, you're all one family."

She looked pained. "You sure shouldn't have said that, mister."

Maebelle put her hand on my mouth and made little hushing sounds. "She'll kill you, too."

By now, I'd figured as much. "How'd you come to shoot him, ma'am?"

Maybe Miss Lutra had already decided to end us, so she saw no harm in easing her burden with a bit of confession. "When Caleb brought her around, I saw what sort she were. I told him no more manitou blood in the family."

I didn't know that word, "manitou." An American word, maybe, for those I thought of as the Good People—the fae.

Miss Lutra continued, "Tis nothing but heartache and trouble when a spirit of the land loves a human. I knew what would become of Caleb. And this girl, too. But he wouldn't listen to me." She nuzzled the pelt in her hand. "Since James William died, I couldn't leave off wanting to return to the water. It's a powerful call."

Maebelle, draped in my coat, stirred and whimpered. She stretched out her hands toward the pelt.

I didn't understand everything, but I understood enough. If a young woman wasn't always what she seemed, an old one like Miss Lutra could have secrets, too. "Where's *your* pelt, Miss Lutra?"

"We can't leave off our nature, can we?" she said. "Jesus heals, but the wounds open up again."

"That city sharpie fella run off with your otter skin?"

She looked pained and nodded. "I tried to keep my faith. Married again. Raised my husband's children. I minded grandchildren. And great-grandchildren. And great-great-grandchildren. I've done lost track of the generations. And always prayed for healing. Prayed for death. But God won't take me. I don't believe He can."

The snow fell, thick and wet. "Jesus sent her—" Miss Lutra directed the gun at Maebelle. "As my deliverance. Her pelt's my way out of this world. I went up to the still to fetch the skin. Caleb wouldn't gimme it. We argued and the shotgun just went off. I was only fixing to scare him."

"An accident." I made soothing sounds. "We should get him out of the snow."

Miss Lutra wasn't listening. "But now, at last, hers will do for me. Thank you, Heavenly Father." The old woman dropped my revolver in the snow and wrapped the animal skin around her shoulders.

Miss Lutra's faith rooted me to the spot. I believed her—she was about to turn into an otter—and I waited for the miracle. But the only change I saw was a layer of snow fall across her hair, her shoulders, and the pelt.

"I can't wear it." Miss Lutra's whisper was so faint, I could barely hear her, despite the snow-wrapped silence of the woods. "Why can't I wear it?"

I came to my senses and scooped the Webley up out of the snow just as Maebelle grabbed for her pelt, knocking Miss Lutra into the water. The old woman wouldn't let go and pulled Maebelle in with her.

Miss Lutra might be old, but she bested Maebelle in weight and reach. Soon she'd subdued her thrashing opponent, Miss Lutra's gnarled hands tight around the young woman's neck as she said, "You're so like me. It has to fit."

I splashed into the water after them and grabbed Miss Lutra's shoulders. "Leave her go." Maebelle bit and twisted, but only succeeded in tightening the old woman's grasp. I grabbed at her fingers. "Would cold-blooded murder be like you too, then?" Pinning Miss Lutra's arms to her side, I held her tight, and Maebelle twisted out of her grasp. I pulled the old lady out of the water onto the snow-covered creekbank.

"Leave me be, boy," said Miss Lutra. "'Tis no business of yours."

"See my—good friend—dead, over there?" I pointed at Caleb with the revolver in my hand.

"That were an accident."

I was numb with the cold and pretty slow, I guess. As I started to get up and put the gun in my shoulder holster, she grabbed it back and menaced Maebelle, who stood in the creek, pelt in hand.

"I feel my skin, you know, calling me from afar," Miss Lutra said. "It's moldering in a chifforobe or the like halfway around the world. It's a gnawing pain, every day."

She climbed the bank, knelt under the oak tree's snowy branches, and turned the Webley to her heart. Her eyes glistened. "I've lived in the promise of eternal life with the Lord Jesus for well over a hundred years. Since the day James William witnessed to me under this very oak and baptized me himself in the creek here. You think God will forgive me?"

I stumbled over to her through the snow and ice. "Suicide's for selfish cowards." Cruel words, but I had strong opinions on the topic. "And a mortal sin."

Miss Lutra nodded. Her eyes were empty. "Help me, boy." She handed me my gun. "You're a good boy."

I tried to piece together my thoughts. And stall. "You're the priest's daughter, from way back when."

Her twisted, knobby hands grabbed mine and pleaded with me. "No one, not even my otter clan, has a life this long. But I'm caught, betwixt and between. You could spare my soul the sin."

I looked up at the sky, the revolver in my hand, and the woman kneeling on the ground before me. "Don't make me, Miss Lutra."

"'Tis a mercy. You know it." She seemed confident I could kill her in cold blood.

I plopped in the snow in front of her and whispered, "Ain't you got any care for *my* soul? Or my murder trial?"

Miss Lutra held my face between her palms. "You feel you's already damned, boy. And so, you *is*."

I knew she was right. My wife, Norah, had seen to that. Selfish to the end. The end at her own hand, but my fault. Always, my fault.

She straightened her wet, bedraggled hair. "I'm ready." She straightened her back and closed her eyes. "Shoot, just shoot."

"Leave off telling me my business." I refused to execute her like a traitor. I'd enough of that duty during the war. I tossed the Webley in the snowdrift and then took the knife out of my pocket and unfolded it as I knelt behind her. She quieted as I guided her head to my right shoulder.

I keep my tools sharp. Nothing worse than a dull knife. Just a bit a pressure under her right ear opened the big vein. A bit more, the artery. Blood spattered my hand and face and dripped down her neck, but I held her tight. "Safe home, Miss Lutra," I said as I slid her body into the water. She'd have liked that. She floated for a moment, ice forming around her as water soaked her clothes.

Perhaps it was a trick of the twilight on the ice, but her body seemed to shrink and shoulders narrow, her nose give way to a pointed snoot, and thick gray fur cover the wrinkled face.

I sat on the creekbank, frozen inside and out. Maebelle came to me and sat very close, huddled in my coat, her pelt clasped to her chest. Before long, a curious otter, then another, then another, came over to nudge at their dead cousin. We sat with Miss Lutra until her body disappeared beneath the water, ice, and snowdrifts.

Obviously, the Judge would have no Otter Springs whiskey for Thanksgiving dinner. And I had a missing old woman and an extremely dead moonshiner to explain to anyone who knew I was in town.

Maebelle helped me hoist Caleb up from the creekbank, and with the donkey and a sled we found in the barn we skidded him to the cabin and then covered him with a blanket on the porch. Quiet and sad, the whole experience had taken the starch out of Maebelle.

We slept as sound as Caleb himself, and for the first time in two years I spent not a restless, three-in-the-morning minute wondering where love ends and betrayal begins.

Maebelle, curled up with her pelt against my back all night, was gone when I woke up the next day. And during that long night, did I think of stealing the selkie's pelt? More like I heard it laugh at me. I felt its promise to warm whatever is left of my soul, but I was resolved to be through with fae females and their hidden agendas.

The next day was bright and frozen. Six inches of fresh snow shone under blue skies. The otters were out in full force, whooping it up as they slid down the bank onto the frozen creek.

I reviewed my options over Miss Lutra's blackberry jam and leftover bread. None seemed particularly smart. In the end, I buried Caleb in the family plot I'd found back up in the woods. The first half inch or so of the ground was frozen, but below that the earth, soft from the rain, yielded easily. It felt good to dig a ditch again. Simple, direct labor that yielded a simple, direct result.

I said goodbye to my first real friend in the States and then washed up the dishes, swept the floor, and burned the place to the ground. I headed back to the city without a word to anyone.

The stewpot? Well, Miss Lutra wanted me to have it.

About The Author

Kathy lives and writes in St. Louis, Missouri, USA. Her short fiction has most recently appeared in the Bards and Sages Anthology *Great Tome of Forgotten Relics and Artifacts (The Great Tomes Series, Volume One)*, with earlier works in *Bards and Sages Quarterly*, *Golden Visions Magazine*, and *Mused Literary Journal. Hippocrene* has published several poems. Follow her on Instagram at kathylbrownwrites and Twitter at KL_Brown. Kathy's blog, *Kathy L. Brown Writes: The Storytelling Blog,* lives at kathylbrown.com.

Discover more Sean Joye adventures with *The Resurrectionist*

T urn here," the Judge said from the back seat as he tapped me on the shoulder. "You're about to miss the prison entrance." Obedient ever, I veered left, the Model T skidding across the melting asphalt only to lurch over the gravel road's ruts. At the sight of a chain gang marching toward us, I slammed the brake, and the tires spewed a cloud of dust into the air. The walking boss—on horseback today, no fool in the summer heat—tipped his hat and hurried them along.

Four denim-clad white men stumbled over the gravel and their chains but managed to hang onto the rectangular pine box they carried. Another inmate, a tall, freckled ginger laden with shovels and pickaxes, hurried behind them.